Three Strikes and You're Out

A Follett Beginning-To-Read Book

Three Strikes and You're Out

Valjean McLenighan

Illustrated by Laurie Hamilton

FOLLETT PUBLISHING COMPANY
Chicago

Library of Congress Cataloging in Publication Data

McLenighan, Valjean.
  Three strikes and you're out.

  (Follett beginning-to-read books)
  SUMMARY: Through negligence a boy loses the magic
hen and tablecloth he is given to help his poor mother,
but he is given a third chance when presented with a
magic stick.
  [1. Fairy tales. 2. Folklore] I. Hamilton,
Laurie. II. Title
PZ8.M17958Th   398.2'1 [E]   80–14020
ISBN 0–695–41462–3 (lib. bdg.)
ISBN 0–695–31462–9 (pbk.)

Library of Congress Catalog Number: 80–14020

International Standard Book Number: 0–695–41462–3 Library binding
                                        0–695–31462–9 Paper binding

First Printing

Once there was a poor woman.
Things were hard for her and her boy.

Hello, Mother.
What's to eat?

Not a thing,
I am sorry to say.

I have had it with being so poor. Go see your aunt. Ask her if she can help us out.

So off went the boy to see his aunt.

7

Now go right
home. Watch
that chicken.
Don't tell what
she can do.

The boy and his chicken came to an inn.

Well, the boy got his room.
But the man knew something was up.
That night he found out what it was.

As soon as the boy went to sleep,
the man changed chickens.

The next morning . . .

The boy went to the man.
It did not do any good.

The boy went back to his aunt.
He told all.

He even called me a clown.

Don't be blue.
You get three strikes
before you're out.

Shirts! Not on your life!
This is not just any
old cloth. Put it down.
Tell it you want
to eat. Then watch
what happens.

The boy did as his aunt said.
At once he had all he could eat.

Now take that cloth and go right home. Don't tell what it can do.

If only the boy had done just that! But no. He stopped at the inn.

Give me a room for my cloth and me.

Well, the man knew something was up.
That night he found out what it was.

As soon as the boy went to sleep,
the man changed cloths.

The next morning . . .

Give me some nice chicken soup.

Oh, boy. I have done it again.

The boy did not even stop at the inn.
He went right back to his aunt.

These things happen. You get
three strikes before you're out.
And speaking of strikes —

I have just the thing for you. Take this walking stick. I will tell you what to do.

Soon the boy was back at the inn.

Good to see you again. Nice stick you have there.

The man could not wait to get that stick.
He did not even care what it could do.
He was greedy. That is what did him in.

Late that night, he went to the boy's room.
This time, the boy was ready.

Strike one!

Strike two!

Ow! Ow! Two strikes are plenty.
I will give you back your bird
and cloth. Take them and that
stick and go home. Please.

The boy and his mother were no longer poor. Every Sunday they gave a party. People came from all over.

There was always plenty to eat. Those
who needed money could ask the chicken.
And the stick took care
of the greedy people.

Valjean McLenighan, author of several books in the Follett Beginning-To-Read Series, is a writer, editor, and producer.

Three Strikes and You're Out uses the 161 words listed.

a	did	had	make(s)
about	do(n't)	happens	man
again	done	hard	me
all	down	have	money
always		he	morning
am		heard	Mother
an	eat	hello	my
and	even	help	
any	ever	her	next
as	every	here	nice
ask		him	night
at	for	his	no
aunt	found	home	not
	from	how	nothing
			now
back	gave		
be(ing)	get	I	
before	give(s)	if	of
bird	go(ing)	in	off
blue	good	inn	oh
boy	got	is	old
but	greedy	it	on
			once
called		just	only
came			out
can		knew	over
care			ow
changed		last	
chicken(s)		late	
cloth(s)		life	
clown		longer	
could		lunch	

party	take	wait
pay	tell	walking
people	thanks	was
pets	that	watch
please	the	well
plenty	them	went
poor	then	were
put	there	what('s)
	these	when
ready	they	who
right	thing(s)	will
room	this	with
	those	woman
said	three	
see	time	you('re)
she	to	your
shirts	told	
sleep	two	
so		
some	up	
something	us	
soon		
sorry		
soup		
speaking		
stays		
stick		
stop(ped)		
strike(s)		
Sunday		